W9-BLF-398

Books by Janice May Udry

WHAT MARY JO WANTED
WHAT MARY JO SHARED
EMILY'S AUTUMN
BETSY-BACK-IN-BED
NEXT DOOR TO LAURA LINDA
IF YOU'RE A BEAR

Mary Jo's Grandmother

JANICE MAY UDRY

Illustrated by ELEANOR MILL

ALBERT WHITMAN & Company, Chicago

Chadron State College Library
Chadron. Nebraska

STANDARD BOOK NUMBER 8075-4984-3; LIBRARY OF CONGRESS CARD 78-126433
TEXT © 1970 BY JANICE MAY UDRY; ILLUSTRATIONS © 1970 BY ELEANOR MILL
PUBLISHED SIMULTANEOUSLY IN CANADA BY GEORGE J. MCLEOD, LIMITED, TORONTO
ALL RIGHTS RESERVED, INCLUDING THE RIGHT TO REPRODUCE
THIS BOOK OR PORTIONS THEREOF IN ANY FORM
LITHOGRAPHED IN THE UNITED STATES OF AMERICA

+
Ud8m

3.00

Doubleday

3-28-71

MARY JO'S GRANDMOTHER

Although Mary Jo's grandmother was quite old, she lived alone in a little house in the country.

Whenever Mary Jo's mother or father told her that she should move into town, Grandmother always said, "I've lived in this house almost all my life and I'm too old to move now. I'm content here."

In the summer when they went to visit, Mary Jo and Jeff waded in the little creek that wandered across the pasture. They picked blackberries.

Mary Jo's father always said, "You still make the best berry pie in the world."

And Mary Jo's grandmother always laughed and said, "You just say that because it's true."

They made blackberry jam and carried the jars into Grandmother's little pantry to store for winter.

Sometimes they all drove over to the river and went fishing. On hot summer evenings, they had supper on the porch—fried fish, roasting ears, tomatoes, and green apple pie.

In the fall, they gathered hickory nuts and black walnuts in the woods. And from Grandmother's garden Mary Jo and Jeff each picked out a pumpkin to take back into town for Halloween.

But after the leaves began to fall from the trees and the days grew colder, Mary Jo's mother and father began to worry. They tried to get Grandmother to move into town.

"You haven't even got a telephone. You shouldn't be living all alone way out here," Mary Jo's mother fretted. "Why, your nearest neighbor is clear beyond the main road."

Grandmother smiled. "Now don't you worry about me. I'm as snug as can be here. Don't you fret about me."

Sometimes Mary Jo's sister had stayed by herself for a few days with Grandmother. And sometimes Jeff had stayed out there, too. This year, for the first time, Mary Jo was going to stay on by herself during part of Christmas vacation.

"It's time I taught her how to sew," Grandmother had said. "Bring your suitcase when you come out Christmas, Mary Jo, and we'll have some sewing lessons."

They always went to Grandmother's for Christmas dinner. Other relatives who lived further away usually came too, and it was all they could do to squeeze together around Grandmother's table.

It was a happy family day, with everybody talking, singing, laughing, and teasing. Sometimes Grandmother's little Christmas tree almost danced off the table when the floor shook.

Hugging a new shawl around her shoulders, Grandmother and Mary Jo, in a new red sweater, waved good-bye to everybody from the porch. After the last car went down the drive in the dusk, it was very quiet.

Grandmother gazed out over the bare trees at the sky. "Snow tonight," she said.

Mary Jo looked again at the new sewing basket her mother had given her. It was filled with needles, pins, and spools of thread. She especially loved the little old-fashioned scissors shaped like a crane. His sharp bill snipped off the thread.

After supper and a piece of Christmas candy for each of them, Grandmother turned out the lights on her little Christmas tree. ("You always go to bed very early at Grandmother's," Jeff had told Mary Jo.) Just before she fell asleep, Mary Jo saw great flakes of snow, like feathers, falling outside the little square window.

Even though Mary Jo woke early next morning, she could already hear Grandmother in the kitchen.

"Beautiful snow, beautiful snow," sang Mary Jo when she looked out the window. The countryside was filled with purest white, and the snow was still falling.

"This is the most snow I ever saw here this early in the winter," said Grandmother, putting biscuits into the oven. "Here, Mary Jo, take these bread crumbs out to the birds while I get some jam from the back pantry."

Mary Jo had to sweep snow ahead of herself so she could walk out on the porch. She swept one corner of the porch and put out the crumbs. Before she was back inside the door, hungry birds were fluttering over them.

Grandmother had not come back from the pantry yet. It was a little room built two steps down at the back of the house. It was cool and dark.

Then, from the open pantry door, Mary Jo heard a moan. Her grandmother called weakly, "Mary Jo!"

"What happened?" said Mary Jo running to the door. She looked down. Her grandmother was lying on the pantry floor. She had tripped and fallen down the steps!

"I can't get up," moaned Grandmother.

"I'm coming! I'll help you," said Mary Jo.

"Take the biscuits out of the oven first," said Grandmother.

Mary Jo hurried to the oven, opened the door, and lifted the biscuits out with Grandmother's new Christmas pot holders. Then she hurried to the pantry. But when Mary Jo knelt beside her grandmother and tried to lift her, Grandmother winced with pain.

"No, Mary Jo, don't try to lift me. I think my ankle is sprained or maybe my leg is broken," she said. "Now I'm in a fine fix!"

Mary Jo wondered how on earth she could move her grandmother.

"It's my left leg. It hurts too much to move it."

"Don't worry, Grandmother," said Mary Jo. She looked around at the dark little pantry. It was not very warm. Mary Jo ran back through the kitchen. She went into a bedroom and pulled blankets and a pillow off the bed. She took them to the pantry, wrapped the blankets around her grandmother, and carefully put the pillow under her head.

"Good girl," said her grandmother. "Thank goodness you are here, Mary Jo. Just let me rest while I think of what to do. I'll be all right. You go and have some breakfast while the biscuits are hot."

Grandmother leaned her head back and closed her eyes.

Mary Jo went to the kitchen and poured some coffee into a cup and took it out to her grandmother. She gently lifted her head so that she could sip the hot coffee.

"Ah, that's good!" said her grandmother gratefully.

Mary Jo went back into the kitchen and while she munched a biscuit, she looked out the window at the deepening snow. "I don't even have my boots here," she thought.

She knew that she must go for help. There was no neighbor next door to call. She knew she must walk to the main road because grandmother had no telephone. And on a day like this, no one would be passing by on the little road where her grandmother lived. She had heard her father say it was about two and a half miles to the main road.

She went back into the pantry. Grandmother opened her eyes.

"I'm going up to the main road for help," said Mary Jo.

"In all this snow?" said her grandmother.

"I can do it," said Mary Jo.

Her grandmother sighed and leaned her head back on the pillow again. "I guess I'll have to let you go, Mary Jo," she said. "Wrap up good and warm."

"Yes, Grandmother," said Mary Jo. "You rest and don't worry."

"I'll be all right. I'm a tough old bird," murmured her grandmother.

Mary Jo found a pair of old boots in a closet. She made them fit by stuffing the toes full of newspaper. She put on two sweaters, a coat, and an old stocking cap.

When she went to ask her grandmother if she needed anything, she appeared to be asleep. Or had she fainted?

Mary Jo hurried out into the snow, making sure the back door was closed.

The snow had stopped falling, but icy wind tossed handfuls of it around the corner of the house and into her face. Mary Jo walked as fast as she could down the long drive. How she wished there were a neighbor close by!

It took her twice as long as it usually did just to reach the old mailbox. The snow in the road was untouched. No truck or car had been along.

Mary Jo trudged toward the main road, lifting her feet high at each step in the old heavy boots. She had never felt so much alone as she did in that cold windy white world. She never even saw a squirrel.

When she finally reached the main highway, Mary Jo could see that no cars had been along there, either. The snow was too deep. Mary Jo's legs had never felt so tired before.

She had to rest before starting to walk to the nearest house.

Then up the road she saw a black speck moving slowly closer. She stared at it. Then she waved.

"It's the snowplow!" she cried. Although no one was there, she wanted to hear the words herself because she was so glad.

It seemed to take forever for the machine to reach Mary Jo. But finally the men saw her and waved. Mary Jo jumped up and down to keep warm, even though her legs were aching.

The driver stopped the snow-plow and leaned over. "What are you doing out here, little girl?"

Mary Jo explained to him what had happened. "Can you call my father in town? His name is William Wood."

"Sure!" said the man. "But what about you? You can't walk all the way back in this."

"I must get back to my grandmother," said Mary Jo.

"Did you ever ride on a snowplow?"

Mary Jo shook her head.

"Here, climb up. We'll clear the road down to your grandmother's and let you off there. Then we'll go on to the next house and phone your father."

"If you hadn't been at the corner," said the man driving the snowplow, "we wouldn't have cleared this side road until tomorrow. We only clear out the main roads the first day after a big snow like this."

Chadron State College Library
Chadron, Nebraska

When Mary Jo got off at her grandmother's drive, she waved good-bye and walked back up to the house. The men on the snowplow said that they would telephone her father from the first house on the main road beyond the corner.

When Mary Jo went into the pantry, her grandmother's eyes were open and she smiled. "How did you get back so fast, child?"

Mary Jo told her about the snowplow. "Mother and Dad will be here in a little while," she said. "All our worries are over now, Grandmother. I'll go heat some soup."

"That sounds good," said Grandmother. "I'm feeling better already. Thank goodness you were here, Mary Jo."

Mary Jo went into the kitchen and tied her grandmother's apron on. She prepared a nice lunch, and she and her grandmother ate it together in the pantry.

Soon after that, Mary Jo looked out the window.

Walking up the driveway she could see her mother and father and Jeff. The doctor was just getting out of his car.

"They're here, Grandmother!" Mary Jo called, and ran to open the door.

About the Author and Artist

Asked when her interest in writing began, Janice May Udry replied, "As soon as I learned to read and write," adding, "Making up poems and stories, drawing pictures and reading became favorite pastimes. They still are."

Mrs. Udry was born in Jacksonville, Illinois—a town children were quick to claim as unique because ferris wheels were built there. Although she had no brothers or sisters, there were grandparents, aunts, and cousins to visit.

Interest in books led to part-time work in the library when Mrs. Udry was a student at Northwestern University. After graduation and marriage to J. Richard Udry, she became an assistant in a Chicago nursery school. Books now took on fresh meaning as she noticed the wonderful new picture books the children so much enjoyed. At the time, she did not guess how many of her stories would be enjoyed by children everywhere.

From Chicago, the Udrys moved to California and eventually to Chapel Hill, North Carolina, where Mr. Udry is a sociologist at the university. The Udrys have two daughters, Leslie and Susan, and their mother notes, "The idea for many of the books I have written began when something one of my daughters did or said reminded me of an incident or a feeling from my own childhood."

Illustrations by Arthur Rackham had a strong appeal for artist Eleanor Mill when she was a child. Her interest in drawing began early, and by the time she had completed high school in Rockville, Maryland, she was ready to enroll at the Corcoran School of Art, in Washington, D.C., for professional training.

Miss Mill has illustrated many picture books and textbooks, but the one she especially chooses as a favorite is *What Mary Jo Shared*. Now married, Eleanor Mill has her studio and home in New York City.